The National Poetry Series

The National Poetry Series was established in 1978 to publish five collections of poetry annually through five participating publishers—Viking Penguin, Persea Books, Atlantic Monthly Press, Copper Canyon Press, and the University of Illinois Press. The manuscripts are selected by five poets of national reputation. Publication is funded by the Copernicus Society of America, James A. Michener, Edward J. Piszek, and The Lannan Foundation.

1989

Tom Andrews, *The Brother's Country*
Selected by Charles Wright/Persea Books

Thomas Centolella, *Terra Firma*
Selected by Denise Levertov/Copper Canyon Press

David Clewell, *Blessings in Disguise*
Selected by Quincy Troupe/Viking Penguin

Roland Flint, *Stubborn*
Selected by Dave Smith/University of Illinois Press

Carol Snow, *Artist and Model*
Selected by Robert Hass/Atlantic Monthly Press

THE PENGUIN POETS
BLESSINGS IN DISGUISE

David Clewell currently lives in St. Louis, where he teaches writing and literature at Webster University.

Blessings in Disguise

Disguise

11-16-00

DAVID CLEWELL

Penguin Books

PENGUIN BOOKS
Published by the Penguin Group
Penguin Books USA Inc.,
375 Hudson Street, New York, New York 10014, U.S.A.
Penguin Books Ltd, 27 Wrights Lane,
London W8 5TZ, England
Penguin Books Australia Ltd, Ringwood,
Victoria, Australia
Penguin Books Canada Ltd, 10 Alcorn Avenue,
Toronto, Ontario, Canada M4V 3B2
Penguin Books (N.Z.) Ltd, 182–190 Wairau Road,
Auckland 10, New Zealand

Penguin Books Ltd, Registered Offices:
Harmondsworth, Middlesex, England

First published in the United States of America by Viking Penguin, a division of
Penguin Books USA Inc. 1991
Published in Penguin Books 1991

10 9 8 7 6 5 4 3 2

LIBRARY OF CONGRESS CATALOGING IN PUBLICATION DATA
Clewell, David. 1955–
    Blessings in disguise/David Clewell.
        p.   cm.
    ISBN 0 14 058.672 5
    I. Title.
  PS3553.L42B58   1991b
   811'.54—dc20   90-7879

Printed in the United States of America
Set in Perpetua
Designed by Ann Gold

Acknowledgments

Grateful acknowledgment is made to the editors of the following publications where these poems first appeared:

BOULEVARD: "Sitting Out the Sadness"
CHOWDER REVIEW: "Dancing Down the Circus"; "Losing My Voice"; "Mormon Graveyard, Utah Night"; "The Distance"
CIMARRON REVIEW: "This Book Belongs to Susan Someone"
THE CREAM CITY REVIEW: "Depot: Beaver Dam, Wisconsin"
DACOTAH TERRITORY: "The Hotel" (as "Gladiola Hotel")
THE GEORGIA REVIEW: "We Never Close"
THE MIDWEST QUARTERLY: "After the Seance"; "The Woman at the Jukebox"
NORTHEAST: "The Dogs"; "The Game"
OTHER ISLANDS: "Storm"
POETRY: "Back to Life"; "New Year's Eve Letter to Friends"; "Two Alley-Songs for the Vegetable Man: St. Louis"
RIVER STYX: "The Lodger" (What Comes Back; Radio; Rising And Falling); "Traveller's Advisory"; "What Other People Think"
STONECLOUD: "The Hardrock Kid"

"After the Seance" was reprinted in *1981 Anthology of Magazine Verse* (Monitor Books, Los Angeles).

"Radio (as "At the Transients' Hotel") was printed as a broadside by Nevertheless Press (St. Louis, 1985).

"The Distance" was reprinted and illustrated by Dave Morice for *Poetry Comics.*

"As Far as the Eye Can See" appeared in a letter-press, limited edition from Nevertheless Press (St. Louis, 1989).

Several of these poems appeared in a chapbook, *The Blood Knows to Keep Moving,* published by Chowder Chapbooks (*Chowder Review,* Wollaston, Massachusetts).

for my father at his drafting table all night engineering his own lines,

who taught me the art of incredible patience and a steady hand

Contents

I THE MAGICIAN'S LUNCH   1

The Magician's Lunch   3

Why the Bird Dropped You, Marlan   6

Heroes   8
    The Dogs   8
    The Game   10
    The Distance   12

Two Alley-Songs for the Vegetable Man: St. Louis   14

The Woman at the Jukebox   18

After the Seance   20

Slides from the Dowsers' Convention   22

Poem for the Man Who Said *Shit*   25

Losing My Voice   27

Sitting Out the Sadness   30

II AS FAR AS THE EYE CAN SEE   37

    In the Backyard   39
    The Communion   41
    The Story of Light   45
    Inheritance   47
    Song in Spite of the Smart Money   49

III   CLOSE TO HOME   51

The Hardrock Kid   53

Depot: Beaver Dam, Wisconsin   55

Storm   57

The Lodger   59
    What Comes Back   59
    Radio   61
    Rising and Falling   62

Dancing Down the Circus   64

Traveller's Advisory   67

Letter from Eureka, Nevada   69

Mormon Graveyard, Utah Night   71

Close to Home   73
    The Clean Plate   73
    The Hotel   75
    The Suicide   77

We Never Close   79

IV   LIKE NOTHING YOU'VE   85
     EVER SEEN

This Book Belongs to Susan Someone   87

What Other People Think   90

Back to Life   92

New Year's Eve Letter to Friends   100

PART I.

The Magician's Lunch

One of the main weaknesses of mankind is the average man's familiarity with the word impossible.

—Napoleon Hill,
Think and Grow Rich

The Magician's Lunch

I.

No one pays their way in anymore
unless it says that you'll read minds
way back in the cheap seats or find
a purple comb at the bottom of a purse
or piece together names and birthdates
dancing in thin air.
The cards I make fly, the fire in my hands,
the dove born out of its own whiteness?
Not enough.
Maybe levitate a body and they'll come up,
slow, out of their reasonable drinks.
So now I do days, half-empty auditoriums,
rows of schoolchildren figuring how it's done.
They just guess what they've been told:
the wires, the plants, the hollow toppers.
Handkerchiefs with five-inch hems.
No one worries when the saw comes down
and threatens the woman into two.

II.

I'd count the day in nickels all week
until Orpheum Saturday morning.
Newsreels marched us closer to war,
but the tin band never failed to show,
sounding Boldini on stage. For an hour

his arms would wing through the air,
wrapping us in, and we applauded
the way he summoned birds and fire,
drew out all the colors he knew.
My eyes were crosshairs beading in
on those hands where a ring on every finger
caught the pale stage lights
and threw back shades of emerald,
of amethyst and ruby. He never said a word
I remember.

III.

The day I ran home,
my mouth filled with the wildest stories yet.
The woman floating above the stage, suspended,
the whole audience breathing her breath.
Out into the backyard and ninety degrees.
My father, locked out of his workshed,
sitting on the steps and cutting new keys
out of the hot afternoon. The buzzing of flies
and me seeing what's wrong.
Waving my arms in front of the door.
Calling out, believing
in my best abracadabra.
My mother at the kitchen window
calling me into lunch, winking at my father like
you know he's excited. And he, disappearing

back into the sweat, the metal taking shape
in his ringless hands. Shaking his head like
the boy's gotta learn it's keys
and common sense what opens doors.

Why the Bird Dropped You, Marlan

Two large black birds with 8-foot wingspans swooped into a backyard in Lawndale, Illinois and took a 10-year-old boy for a twenty-foot ride, his mother said yesterday.

—from a newspaper story

You're just finding out
what you don't need to believe. 70 pounds,
not enough yet in the world to realize
what your screaming said. To your mother
waving her own arms like wings,
wanting the world to slow down for a second.
To the bird, scared in its prehistoric brain,
just playing with you and the experts who would say
no North American bird like this.
What could you know
over the beating of wings, of birdheart
and your own heart flapping out the ribcage,
over softness of breastfeathers tousling your hair?

Your weight? Not too much for this bird.
Not the scream flying out your small mouth.
Maybe the bird itself, feeling its own hugeness
crowding the day, too suddenly unexpected.
Lifting you like another feather
but straining the limits broad daylight allows.
At night with no one watching
you could have gone farther,
you and this great bird together
no longer a bundle of uneasy grace.

Moving in and out of the dark all night
until breakfast, and your mother calls you down
and you come from wherever you are.
Anything less conspicuous
than a Midwest summer afternoon!

From now on you'll hear a thousand answers to
no question. When you talk with your friends
and the reporters come flocking,
stick to your ten years,
all the facts they want to know.
Later, in color encyclopedias,
you can look for names that fit
the jetblack wings, the 12-inch head,
the rings around the neck and the claws
that came down on your shoulders and had you,
Marlan, had all of them going for awhile.

Heroes

I. THE DOGS

In my town people said
dogs barked their heads off every summer.
I used to stare at every dog and wait.
I'd drown the heat in a bottle of pop,
watching Mazzetti pumping gas.
Old men came by to hash over the weather
and he'd hide underneath a Plymouth and curse.
Once when he was making easy change,
I asked if he'd ever seen
a dog bark its head off. He said
it just seemed that way sometimes,
like they could if they wanted to.
That day the old men thought
the sky looked like rain,
they hoped so, we could use it.
I laid my bottle in
with a hundred other empties and decided
in this town dogs couldn't,
even if they wanted.

After that I stayed up nights,
saw the way lights went quiet
one by one, then out in all the houses.
Trains hummed past midnight to another day.
Did the mayor sleep with bigger ambitions?
Did the bagboy from the grocery dream a day

his thin arms would lift love? Up in bed
my hands invented shadows on the wall.
With practice they got good:
dark shapes of filling stations,
trees lining darker streets.
When I twisted my body a certain way
I could make the hospital where I was born.
I made my own face in one of its windows,
looking out, just barely alive.
I made a parade go past.
I put someone in the back of a sedan,
excited and waving. From that window,
nosed to the glass in a nurse's arms,
it seemed like he could have kept on going,
could have been waving good-by.

II. THE GAME

Friday nights the town eats early.
Lights flood the field and bleachers fill
with people cheering themselves on.
Any team from out of town
is good enough to lose.
The taste of sweat at lip's curl
is enough, reminds them
something's on the line.
Mazzetti reaches for the fences,
uniform drenched in this good life.
Junkman Turner knows throwing strikes all night
is worth 500 cans clanking empty before noon.
They have been dreaming all winter of this:
the home run trot, the perfect game.
The players chatter the air into frenzy
while the crowd yells its heart out
where they can see it.
They play the game over in the tavern
past midnight until the last song
spins out of the jukebox, snapped up
in the din as they throw themselves out.
To where car doors slam, keys turn
toward home in their ignitions.

All the way back the radio is ecstatic
with the news. He smiles, tugs at his shirt,
the letters of the town heating his chest

the way love used to.
He brakes up in the driveway and strikes
a match, a small bargain of light.
He sees his wife's face, quiet
as she leaves the car, moving
without looking back into the house
until he's lost her. His fingers burn
and bring him back to the big game,
another night he's come out on top of.
He's learned the hero's words, to say
how it was nothing when he knows
different, how it must be something
to wind up in the dirt so many times
and sliding, ahead of any throw
or daylight or thought of turning back.
Sliding into home through the dark,
thinking *safe,* in the middle of his life.

III.   THE DISTANCE

The letters still come once a month,
full of the same faces in the street.
Full of clothes hanging out to dry,
of picnics everyone is part of.
And now they tell me wind chimes
over the front door, I'd love them,
they just know it.

Tonight I sit on the porch at the end of winter
and watch trees collecting leaves.
Stars heating up the sky.
Thinking ahead they burn small holes,
leaving themselves a way out.
I wonder how to raise my voice from so far,
spinning hundreds of miles away.
Another planet they can't imagine life on.
Here there are people in the street
with names I just don't know.
Every letter closes with
we'll keep a light on for you.
When I go back inside someone will ask me
for the latest news, and I will tell her this:
that the temperature is climbing
out of the cold ground, that the dogs
are learning to bark again.
That all the trains in the world might stop running,
the engineers piling out of their cabins

to stare down the tracks at
the worst that could happen.

The letters still come once a month,
each one begging the same question.
I keep meaning to say how I miss things,
how I'll be back to say hello
while something in the back of my throat
answers no the best it can.
When I sleep the wind turns
into desperate voices. Hollow bones
hung together by threads
drum a message in my ear: *this
is what we have to make the best of.*
But outside, flowers break new ground.
Take root. Begin to grow.
In a distance, clothes still flapping
on a line strung through the dark.
There's a light still on for me.
I'm learning to live with it.

Two Alley-Songs for
the Vegetable Man: St. Louis

I.

I've never seen the vegetable man
but I know his litany and his bells
as he negotiates the alley mornings
when the sun's a bad idea coming up again.
I've tried to sleep right through him
but I've heard his customers
piling down fire escapes
and waving their thick hands:
the woman up from Fayetteville
whose robe is always undone.
The fat man in love with bad cigars
who beats his dog when his check runs thin
and none of his numbers come up right.
Dozens of my neighbors abandoning their beds
and filling the alley with vegetable frenzy.
They go down to marvel
at the resiliency of lettuce, the humility
of corn, the artichoke's high-mindedness.
They can't see or hear me rooting around
in my own dark garden of sleep.
They're busy being lifted
on the green wing of his song.

It might be all right, his song and dance,
if this were storybook Europe years ago
and I was staying with some kind family
hiding me from the town constabulary. Maybe

then I could take some comfort in his singing,
could thank him underneath my breath
for another day's auspicious sign.
But there's always a price on local color
this late in the century's season
where there's never enough sleep
to undo the day before
and the cartoon dog who guards our sleep
spins around and around on his leash.
Here comes another day
of fragile commerce in the world.
We want infinite wisdom,
and somebody sells us potatoes. Unbelievably
out of love, we settle for tumescence.

I dream about tipping over his cart.
I'm setting it on fire and I'm laughing
while his produce rolls away free.
He'll never know it could be worse,
how every time I wake up colorless
and hungry at noon, the day already
picked over for the brightest plums, I think
maybe tomorrow I'll leave my long bed
and yell down for a pound or sack of
what everyone else is having.
And he might turn his blank face up
and wonder where the hell I've been
all his life. For me he's been saving
the frivolous turnips,

15

the cantaloupe's orange melancholy,
the ineffable sadness in the onion's heart
that's mine, all mine, for a song.

II.

Here's to courage when the alley runs out
and the vegetable man sings his long way home.
That his children eat everything
that threatens to go bad and they grow wiser.
That the knife of his honest living
steels itself in its sheath by his bed.
That for him it continues to be this simple,
paring things down to their essential gist:
stalk and seed, pulp and core.
It's a faith that could sustain us too
if only we could see it steaming from the soup,
leaking from the colander,
shining round and hard in bowls
on tables we all set, hoping.
It's the charm we need to string around our necks
when the alley cuts its teeth after dark,
when the fat man and his dog are talking
the common language of scream
and a woman is naked, crying in her window
while the wrong song comes out of the radio
and someone we don't know is running,
looking over his shoulder
as far as he can back into his life

and seeing it all in this one reflexive moment,
this last dispatch from the heart going out.

We need the man with his vegetable song
who's already dressing himself in the dark
to make it back another day
and wake us with the only love he knows
so we can say over and over and mean it
like the edge of his knife means its sure business,
like his own children mean each morning they're alive:

there's nothing in another night
the color of bruise, if it comes tonight,
can harm us.

The Woman at the Jukebox

She calls the change in her hand her own
another minute before she lets go.
Her fingers read every song.
When she tosses her hair, she knows
what could come next: drinks stacking up
at the bar in her name. An offer
to dance. Maybe she's glad
when nothing happens.

The 8-ball cracks through the crowd
where a lawyer's doing card tricks.
He says pick any one, but only certain things
count lucky. Nothing's for sure.
If the 4-horse shows, if the White Sox win,
someone's bound to be happy.

The woman at the jukebox,
on the edge of music, isn't sad.
The quarters drop and she makes her choices.
Her alphabet of songs lights the board.
She smiles back to her seat
past the boy working the Snow Queen
for a free one, past cigarettes falling
down and out of the machine.

While the songs keep spinning
her night's on a string and she hums, soft.
Her fingernail digs a rough heart in the bar.
To get this far she's come from somewhere,

someone's daughter. Say her marriage busted
or she never married,
that she's passing through town
or she's lived here all her life.
She leaves the same way she came in,
heels clicking sharp across the floor.
The quietest man in the place kicks himself
under the table, watches her out the door.

The bartender puts the bottles back in rows
and thinks for now things couldn't be better,
knows *maybe* the 4-horse and *maybe* the White Sox.
In his heart he knows that luck runs
hot and cold in streaks. He pulls the plug
and the jukebox goes dead.
He drums his fingers on the radio, waiting
for the first good news to break.

After the Seance

Cars disappearing from the driveway,
carrying their cargo of vague hope.
Three times a week
she stands behind the shades and waits.
When the last lights tail away
she pulls down another night of rigging.
The tambourine, her father's once from show days.
The fan whose low speed blows the spirits through.
The tape recorder in a drawer, humming
dead silence now.
Her part is the practiced sweat, the eyes
sealed closed and dumb. This is the Next Life
that comes easy.
Working up the voice is harder. Learning
how to beat a stranger's ears into believing.

The circle of hands has broken, gone home
to dark houses. Her own hands
pour coffee in a cup, count money
out of an envelope on the way upstairs.
Twenty dollars for Aunt Clara, fleeting,
taken by surprise in sleep. Another ten
for someone's Jacob, blown out at 80 MPH.
Whatever was agreed on is all accounted for.

In her room she undresses her life,
sees the way it could have looked: married,
respectable daughters, Connecticut and snow.
All her closest friends are dead

and she's convinced herself again
no life beyond this one.
The radio on her table goes static
and she swears, can't get any station clear.
The only voice she hears is hers, growing
slowly louder. *Give me*
something to hold onto,
some jewelry, a shred of clothing.
We close our eyes. We show our faith.
Who'll be my spirit guide tonight?

Slides from the Dowsers' Convention

Although dowsing through the ages has been associated with the search for water with a forked stick, the so-called divining rod, the means and ends have expanded broadly in recent years.

—from the keynote address

I.

Maybe that explains this exhilarated matron
wielding her husband's flannel pajamas
and offering insomniacs cures for a dollar.
In the noise all that's heard is
that her husband's never failed.

II.

Then this man with one arm
and a coat hanger that will pinpoint
your war wounds for a loved one.
You are unnerved when you hear
he will use his own discretion.

III.

In the back of the hall, the town's mayor
growing smaller. Someone from the coast
used a bottle of wine
to find his oldest daughter
last night at 2 A.M.

IV.

On days like this crude maps are persuasive.
Lots of arrows. You could be anywhere.
Successful finds are blown up
on an overhead projector. There's
the mayor's daughter, sitting pretty.

V.

The keynote speaker drones on dryly.
His voice cracks like parched earth.
He is dealing in facts. He sweats,
makes it clear the glass of water
in his hand is only a beginning.

VI.

At dinner the dowsers parade to the river.
These are the old ones, returning
to the source. There is no doubt
in their minds. Those sticks are bucking
wishbones in their hands.

VII.

Here they are, up all night
trading secrets. They fill the hall

to overflow. They drive hard bargains with the skeptics that float in, making believers of themselves all over again.

Poem for the Man Who Said Shit

At first I lost it in your beard
so I took a guess, told you the time.
You stepped closer and let it fly,
again and again, a single syllable,
a voice swollen with the confidence
that comes from years of study.
You gestured every way at once
like everything was part of some long story
you forgot all the words to but one.
By the time you waded into traffic,
your salvo booming louder,
I finally got it right and thought
why not, we all make what we know look easy:
high pressure systems, finite mathematics,
the impossible jumpshots we turn in our sleep.
And tonight if the filmclip makes the news,
a doctor will come on, swivelling
behind a sturdy desk, his mouth full
of polished stones like *childhood* or *the war*
or his favorite, *urban stress.*

If you're lucky down at the station
this won't take too long.
You go over and over your only story until
finally it could be anything, lost
on too many trips to the brain: *Lawnmower.*
Watermelon. The rookie cop is worried
he's losing his first bust.
The sergeant's been around, knows

even though he's got a family to think of
there's nothing he can do. When you leave,
he'll tell the rookie a long story,
how it's too bad the way the world is.
Me, I'm the witness who wouldn't swear
to anything. When I leave
the sergeant will say it's people like me.

Losing My Voice

I.

The memory of holding a shell
tight to the ear's lip
and hearing the sounds inside
where the whole ocean fit:
lap of wave, hiss of drying sand.
Funny the sea never at stormtide,
yap of undertow dragging gravel,
dredging up bottom.
Always the water
clearer than your memory of it.
The sun keeping its eye out,
scouring the beaches white and safe.

Now the memory of the shell itself,
a dry bone in your hand. The animal
long gone, overgrown or dead.

In your mind pick it up again.
Listen for the swell of ocean there,
drowning the darker side. Think
how pretty this shell, this sea.
This haunted house of air.

II.

In the morning one morning it's gone
without word. In its place I inherit

a collection of wheezes nesting in my larynx.
I look in the mirror at what I want to say
and see strange eggs pushing up my throat,
breaking in my mouth.

In the street everyone wants me to
come again. I find ways to suggest to them
I'm doing all I can.
The woman in the grocery makes me rasp *honey*
half a dozen times until she's certain
it's just small talk.

Brute force doesn't bring it back.
I bang my chest until my hands turn into
conciliatory gestures.
The remaining words go deeper,
humming among themselves. In my head
I deftly step through sentences, through
nuance and inflection. But
what comes out is the sound wind makes
through a paper bag blown out.

Why do they choose now to get me going?
Long distance calls, people at my door
with clipboards wondering what I think.
I whisper to them all I've lost it,
that I can't say what's to blame.
I've thought about that too
while taking well-intended cures.

Now honeyed lungs, now salted tonsils.
When I swallow
a tea bag rises and falls in my throat.

III.

In a field, a woman digging potatoes.
The wind blows something in her ears
before evening. She stands up straight,
eyes into the trees. It's nothing,
at least nothing she can say.
She bends back to her work
filling baskets with potatoes.
Yanked from the soil and sleep they know,
they stay quiet in their skins,
in their vegetable rage. Giving away
nothing of the whiteness that burns inside.
The pulp, the heart,
the thing that sustains them:
what the woman can't hear.
All there is to say.

Sitting Out the Sadness

I never dance to sad songs. When I'm on stage and I hear music, I feel it way inside me. And songs like that don't ever make me feel like dancing.
                    —Venus, exotic dancer at the Yellow Rose

FOR ALBERT GOLDBARTH

The way she lets down her waist-length hair
you'd think she had a lover waiting
in a room at the end of a long hallway,
not some DJ in the middle of his cornball
introduction, falling back on lines he's used
a hundred times before, lines
a place like this is perfect for. This time
it's the one about the heavenly body
that does a whole lot more than take up space.
And here comes another unmistakable love song
for all the hard-of-loving among us,
bass line pounding every stray conversation
into whisper and less, into smoke
thinning into the pale shafts of light
until the whole room is Venus, Venus,
Venus, leaning hard into her music,
her body one long muscle of unmitigated joy.

If there's one doleful note or desolate lyric,
any song weighted down with the baggage of sorrow,
that's someone else's dance.
She grabs her shoes and leaps off the stage
oblivious to the grace in even this,
her practiced getaway. And although

we've seen it all night with our own eyes,
it's a luxury we still don't know,
this sitting out the sadness.
She's already making her way to the bar, worrying
a cigarette, unravelling a string of small talk
from table to obligatory table. She could be
a sudden cousin we never knew we had,
you and I are that polite. She squeezes
between us, a hand on our shoulders, and says
she thinks it's a miracle
anyone can dance to a song like this one.
She guesses someone's got to do it.
Someone's asked for it. Someone always does.
If you ask me what's miraculous
it's that we're talking the perplexities of music
with a woman in one brief grace note of clothes.
You're telling your own version of the marvelous,
how so many people can continue to believe
that the *Titanic* was adrift in buoyant song
even as it headed for the floor of the sea.

Now that's a likely story she's never heard before.
She's never heard of the *Titanic,* but don't we think
it's possible it really happened that way,
just a little possible?
Tell her that was one survivor's story,
something that may have made it easier for him
to keep on going. He remembered running,
remembered a woman shouting the one thing

she must have been suddenly sure of. But what came next
he couldn't remember, how he ended up
in a boat by himself floating free.
When he claimed he heard the people still on board
singing hard, some last gigantic act of faith,
he was lying through his teeth
for a reason: the rest of his life.

We've known people with their own stories
of making it out alive.
Out of recent history, out of yesterday
and the day before, small boats going down
with all their fragile cargoes.
If there was any music, it's faded,
lost in memory's white noise:
the one light humming through the night
on the top floor of the rooming house.
The ringing phone at 4 A.M. calling someone out
of bed and into the middle of someone else's
bad dream that just won't quit.
The whistle in the arc of the headache ball
taking aim each day at whatever's still left
standing in the middle of our own unlikely lives.

Better it should happen that way, better faded
than a tune that gets stuck in our heads
and we can't shake it, and we know
at the worst moment possible
we might burst into song, like a flower

or like a flame, but without the luxury of saying
flower, I'll only do a flower.
Because we are not afforded choices.
Even though the song somewhere way inside us,
if we could make it out at all, might not
make us feel like dancing. Even though we'd rather
bargain for assurances, no matter how imperfect,
from any perfect stranger strong enough to smile.
As if that music had nothing to do with us.

A place like this is a comforting thought
to take some refuge in: it's never anything
personal. Just when you think
this conversation's warming up,
here comes the Hospitality Kiss
thinning on your lips in less time
than the ice melting into your drink.
Just think how the needle never sticks
or skips, precision we're simply not used to.
Just ask Venus, rising in the dark
around our table, now a disembodied voice
telling her favorite farewell joke. How
she has to run now and put on some clothes
because her whole career is taking off.
What's funnier than that
is how it's always easier going
when you know by heart what song comes next,
when you know what turn is yours and exactly

what you'll do when you take it. And how far.
And in the mundane light
of a day in the world like every other day
it should always be as easy
as some DJ's mindless patter filling the empty spaces,
killing time until we're ready
to go on with whatever we've got.
And if anything went wrong, if anyone
broke an unspoken rule, some thin skin of decorum,
the bouncer would heft up out of his chair
in the middle of our living room,
300 pounds of menace on our side for once.

Think how easy the going would be
with some perpetual soundtrack playing our whole lives
and when we were about to turn the wrong corner
the music would come up, obvious
and threatening and we could hear it coming
and race back to the bar for a drink
to forget one more close brush with the credits
and that sad music they'd stoically roll through
rising, disappearing into that irrevocable dark.

Here in the flickering dark of the Rose
what passes for sadness is nothing sad:
the strobes gone blue, some slow song
more bad than wistful winding down,
a room full of anxious people waiting

for Venus to come out again. Venus,
incandescent, limber in her skin. Venus
who makes it her business to realize
the pure implausibility of sadness,
who dances the mere thought into thin air.
Maybe there's more good in this
than we can get around to feeling.
The DJ's talking it up, he'd say, like
there's no tomorrow. He'd mean that
in the best way he could imagine.
Not that tonight is the end of the world
as we've suddenly come to know it all over,
but that tonight keeps on going, maybe never
ends, that there's no more sooner
or later to go off sadness' deep end,
no more days we don't feel much
like dancing but we dance.
No more chance of the heart
emptying its chambers, a salvo of sadness
that could blow this or any room to smithereens.
Not with Venus, glistening in the altogether
under tin foil stars pasted on the too-low
ceiling that passes for heaven tonight.

The DJ asks us all to put our hands together
for the lady. And we do.
The left hand and the right hand,
that live their whole lives on opposite sides
of every story, in the extremes of all

and nothing at all, are thinking of us
at the end of another day's long haul
when they meet somewhere in the expanse between
it doesn't get any better than this and
it doesn't get any better than this
to work out their judicious compromise,
this show of strength, their wild applause.

PART II.

As Far as
the Eye Can See

As Far as the Eye Can See

I believed until now that all the things of the universe were inevitably fathers or sons.

—Cesar Vallejo

FOR JOE GONNELLA

I. IN THE BACKYARD

On summer nights my father would sit still
watching the sunset over the house give up
to the beginning of the dark.
When stars burned through he thought of counting
but the numbers never came as fast as stars.
He shook his fists. The fireflies winked.
He'd walk over to the garden, thinking
what could grow there: tomatoes, lettuce, beans.
A way of saying he had plans,
and he cursed the flowers for coming back another year.

That long fall doctors called it a miracle
each day his brain shrugged off more cells
and kept on humming.
Each night he prowled the backyard and made his stand
against the houseful of strangers,
their mouths full of love
and patience and other smaller treasons.
He filled his pockets with notes to himself:
every smile's a loaded gun.
He'd read them to moles he imagined in the hedges.
He covered himself with leaves and sang *Amazing Grace*

until his voice got dry and thin.
When the leaves turned to snow
he declared his private war on the planet
and hurled his body at the ground again and again.

He knew what came next was the kitchen light,
a beacon calling him a long way home.
A face at the window hoping he'd come, praying
his heart's low droning would steer him
one more time through that kingdom of angels
frozen in the snow.

II.   THE COMMUNION

One day when I came home from school
my mother stopped her sweeping long enough
to tell me he was *gone*. At first I thought
she meant he'd wandered off again and did I know
of any secret place to find him this time.
I had no idea. I was thinking
of anywhere I hadn't tried before
when she broke down crying in my arms.
She meant gone for good
and it came to me out of nowhere, the word
she couldn't bring herself to say,
the word that was already turning her world
into a small room she couldn't sweep clean.

And I was jealous, I wanted to know for myself
the sudden difference his dying made.
I wanted to take it in my hands and feel it
chafe or burn or soothe. But I went numb
and couldn't feel a thing. It scared me
when I didn't even feel my mother
hanging on while her grief kept coming,
waves breaking over the hull of her heart.
So I took water from the kitchen sink
and drew a thin line down my cheek
when she wasn't looking. To make a better
show of it. As if to say she wasn't
alone, that I knew what she must feel,

that we could talk each other through this
if she'd trade some of her grief for some of
mine, with no real salt or bluster in it.

Years later and we're still talking, but
these days the last things in our eyes are tears.
I go back to visit every chance I get,
and I always end up making the same promise:
to take a fistful of flowers to his grave.
For my mother that's a way of life, a genuine
communion. And I envy her strong faith in
those songs she sends to heaven in his name.
Amazing Grace, of course.
And one I never liked, *Just As I Am.*
I envy the peace she's made with his dying,
how it's become a garden she lovingly tends.
She wants that for me too, but all I make
are promises I won't keep
so she can worry less about the straw
falling out of the broom, about the house
settling a few more inches this year.

His grave's no place I ever would have thought
to look, but he's always there for her.
No matter what. That's the part I envy most.

• •

Today when she drew a rough map of the grounds
and marked his plot with an X, I really believed
this time it would be different:
I'd get in the car and give it gas
and not let up until I made it all the way out there,
where finally I could be as good as my word.
Because part of me wanted to say one time
I'd gone the whole ridiculous distance,
followed my mother's treasure map, dug deep
through layers of memory, and still
I'd come up empty-handed.

But I'm relieved and secretly happy every time
drinking in the afternoon, The Idle Hour Lounge,
a good mile shy of the cemetery.
They know my story here. And even if
it's been a year, when I walk through that door
they know I've made it back this far again,
that it won't be long until I'm paying for
a few too many fingers of the usual
and handing the flowers to the first woman
who doesn't ask me for an honest explanation.

Today her name's Michele, and both of us
have other things we could be doing.
That's why people sit at bars in daylight.
Whiskeys later when we're leaning on the jukebox
and finishing a kiss, she looks the music over

for something slow so we can dance.
And suddenly I have a desperate need for
any song called *Make Me Better Than I Am.*

No matter what happens next,
let it come as a blessing.
And if it has to be a blessing in disguise,
let it be more obvious than usual:
false nose and glasses, a cockeyed hat. Anything
that won't take much too long to recognize.

III. THE STORY OF LIGHT

I remember staring through the telescope
your father gave you when you begged him.
He showed us how everything seemed closer,
bigger than it was.
On nights with no moon in them
we aimed at lighted windows, looking for
constellations of girls we hadn't seen before.
One night overgrown with stars
he collapsed on the porch in the middle of his life
and left our questions hanging dumb in the air:
what are stars made of, how big are they really?
We knew all about wishing
but we didn't know where to start.

After the funeral we learned names:
Sirius the Dog Star. Ursa the Bear.
Debbie Fuller the long-legged blonde.
We drew charts and diagrams, made plans
to see our way clear.
We weren't old enough to know the story of light,
how fast it can move
and still be so long coming, how it comes
at once from what's dead and what's alive.
We still can't tell the difference
between first light and last
when it rummages through our sleep
or sits down in the parlor

or waits behind the curtains we draw in the bedroom
until we finally come up out of women we love for air.

Your father's eyes are flickering stars
fixing themselves in your sky.
Remember how light's measured in years
you never would have dreamed. And maybe it's time
to swear off wishing forever,
time to curse them in their distance,
in their shimmering aberrations. Curse them
for rising cold from your belly every night
to name the two of you one in the blood.
Curse the life they shed light on.
Curse the story of light.

Better to see what they should have become.
Make them stones you would sink straight down in water,
make them gristle in the soup.
Make them dull coins covering the eyes,
not eyes, not stars burning their white apologies,
not anything you've waited for, not ever.

IV.   INHERITANCE

You and I used to talk for hours about
how things might have turned out differently
if our fathers had belonged a little more to us
before we *lost* them, another strange word
we learned to say. In our minds
we'd try them on again like the idea of gloves
we guess we would have grown to love.

These days we'd rather talk about our lives
the way they've really been. Sometimes
we take them too personally: the occasional
rattle in your chest that makes you nervous,
why I get upset each time I lose my train of
thought. And when we catch each other in the act of
flirting with the ludicrous, we laugh so hard
we can barely breathe. We blame it on
the only facts we had to start with:
the Dentist, his abscessed heart.
The Draftsman, his brain with crooked lines.
No wonder that we're friends.

We've worked hard for what we've found out since,
and we still call each other when we stumble
on the smallest new detail: a trap door
in the attic back East, the stash of magazines
and stale tobacco. 78s in a junkshop
with your last name on the sleeves.

An obscure uncle who calls from the airport
between flights and refers to something
he assumes I knew only too well.
We share our discoveries as if they belonged to us
both, as if they were bits of arcane lore
we'd tricked into the daylight.

We're curious about anything that shows up
in our faces, in how we shake our heads and laugh
or stab our fingers into the air.
Why I'm drawn to magicians and old hotels,
why you'd always rather take the long walk home.
Anything that might help us
to sort the rumors passed on in the blood
and factor them minus or plus,
to make our own lives a more exact science.
What we don't know could fill books,
and we still go to sleep at night trying to read
every story backwards.

Our official inheritance:
your father's winter scarf, my father's fedora.
We'll put them on when we know more about the rest.
We don't need yet another unconfirmed report
that we're our fathers' sons. Especially when
instead it seems that we were born to be brothers,
hapless initiates in the Holy Order of
Everything That Goes Without Saying.

V. SONG IN SPITE OF THE SMART MONEY

I hammer your laughter
into your cradle.
—J.G., *Poems for My Son*

Joe, the next time you stay up late
drinking in the only place that's open,
don't worry about your imaginary son
tunnelling his long way out of the future.
Right now he could be crawling through the day
your own heart closes down for good.
If he stops to rub a lucky stone,
if he makes a wish,
it's nothing you can hear and you know better,
how everywhere sons keep trying
not to give themselves away.

Trust to your glass half full of bourbon,
the constellation of loose change
splayed on the bar's dark wood.
Nights like this the smart money's on stories
whose endings we can live with:
the lame cast off their crutches
and collapse in the dirt.
The princess has to settle for the village idiot.
It's true every day we know more or less what's coming
but we keep singing our cities to sleep
with songs about how anything could happen.

••

In this one
the heart is a kite
climbing on a long string of blood.
Every atom in the body burns off the weight
of too many years in the planet's shade.
We've never been so light in our lives.
Later we'll practice what to say
in the brilliant world we'd given up for dead.
For now it is enough to know
the wind is kicking up stiff in our favor
and the color coming back to our faces is real

and we're already lifted, already carried away.

PART III.

Close to Home

*Memory is like a shotgun
kicking you near the heart.*
　　　—Frank Stanford

The Hardrock Kid

Nothing could be more wonderful for a hobo than to cross over the Jordan while sleeping in a park.

—Steamtrain Maury

In a sketch he'd fall right in
with the lines of the tree he lies against.
Flicking off mosquitoes, naming each one
for a town with a face he'd recognize.

Some young softball kid
lays into a fat one,
sends it skyward. Hardrock follows
until eyes close and night sounds
hum his body home. Half a century
and he knows the trains are faster,
days longer when the body slows. Still
small secrets get him by, like ways
the blood knows to keep moving.

Squeezes shut his eyes so tight
a hundred headlights prick the black
and he picks one, imagines
a rumbling familiar as breath.
Times his jump but doesn't
jump. This time, Sunday,
no reason to move. He's gone
over and over his brain, every fold
in the map of his country.
He feels the red bandana in his pocket

balled up, clenched
like a fist or a heart.

Under the last moon he remembers
there are secrets he keeps
to himself. That the lazy fly ball
has finally fallen and gone home
is one.

Depot: Beaver Dam, Wisconsin

So small there's barely room for the phone
to ring. Each time it does someone's trying
to save me. My frustration conjures
the worst: a bus curled up on the shoulder
of a road. The ticket man is brimming
with small town sense. He tells everyone
it'll be here when it gets here.
The woman on the other end
of my ticket doesn't hear.
She tosses her hair and heads home.

He puts a hand on my shoulder, the way
he's learned to comfort strangers. Whistles
a secret in my ear: I should learn
to be more patient; he believes
reincarnation. Snow inches up to the door.
A bus horn blares for the hundredth time
in my head, and he tells me how it is:
one fifty a week for changing bulbs
and quarters. Says he has a way of knowing
he can trust me, wants me to believe with him
the sky is full of spirits
on their way to new bodies.
I tell him I'll try to. He's anxious
to go on. I see myself in the station window,
thinking of explaining all this when
I get back. The ways we see ourselves through
when a bus breaks down or a life

goes broke, and waiting is the asking
of the prayer and the answer.

If the soul never dies, then some nights
it's close. No lights for miles and the sky
full of snow. Burning in another town
is a woman who turns in her sleep, who has
no way of knowing the ticket man is talking
in circles of lives that keep on going.
That I'm running my own story up and down
my tongue until I'm sure I'll be convincing.
No way of seeing the two of us going,
our separate ways, for broke.

Storm

We unfold napkins and bolt down dinner.
The radio's full of the storm
and we know the twitch of electricity
here out on the porch, waiting,
iced tea sweating in our summer hands.

Hosing down a lawn giving up to brown
a neighbor yells this'll be a real clapper,
he can tell, we should have seen the walleye
hitting hard all afternoon.

When we came to Wisconsin they told us
about the summer storms thundering
across the lakes and through backyards,
washing weeks of heat down the gutters.
We'd been through rain before,
never realizing how polite.
In this open land, miles of no relief,
the Elks scatter home with their softballs.

Tonight in dark circles around our eyes
another storm gathers. A year of plans
folded into maps stashed on the dashboard.
This house packed up behind us
shifts its new weight in the dark.

Maybe we need the sky falling in once more
to yell *no turning back*.
So let it rain,

drops giving way to sheets of water.
If the roads wash out we'll make it anyway.
If lightning strikes
we'll jump into each other's arms.

We know it won't be long now:
someone with a newspaper full of rain
running down the sidewalk, running home.
This time it will be for everyone's sake
when we hope it isn't far.

Tonight if a tree falls we'll still be here
to hear it, to leave the porch
and dance in the branches
until we're soaked to the skin
and what's underneath comes up to stay alive.

The Lodger

I. WHAT COMES BACK

The way his mirror catches sunlight today
says there was another time and for a minute
he's willing to take it on blind faith.
He knows nothing ever comes back right.
When he recalls the nightclerk
who brought up whiskey, two cigars in humidors,
he can't see through the blue smoke
to the gap-toothed grin, the cracked skull
when they found him on the stairs days later.

He summons up the train that ran along the river,
the towns it made desperately possible.
He wanted to be sure he'd mean *for good.*
He still sees the brakeman's wave turning cruel
in the years the train stopped running through.
And then the woman in the sports car, blonde,
top down, a good green wind up from the South
and he remembers how the nerves went soft,
how the blood rushed a message to his head
that for one day at least he could live forever.
Sometimes in his sleep he hears her
gunning up Main and he could die.

Today his clock will lose a few more minutes,
an act of love he's learned to count on.
But when the sun drops down into the river
it's no falling star, no secret sign,
no reason for saying anything but this:

just another day rolling over, spent.
Next comes the moon, that dusty mirror.
He has to laugh. He remembers some things right.
How the moon rises through the dark,
its pale faith a small wonder
bending home its parcel of light.

II. RADIO

Sunday nights the ancient Philco carries him away.
Familiar stations disappear in the air
and he can pull in towns he's only heard of.
Tonight, Susan Someone in Poughkeepsie
naming her best lovers, the whole city of Cheyenne
sending out tunes to the Hammerhead
deep in his haul to Aberdeen. The mayor's up late
in Sandusky taking questions from people with dogs.
Buoyed by the weather report in Tacoma
he rattles off the names of the entire Gashouse Gang
but the Pontiac goes to some kid who's only close.

—

It's a night of strange connections:
flying saucers, mutant strains of VD,
the threat of war and celebrity birthdays
and now the gospel man
who lives at the top of his lungs.
For the hell of it he joins the radio in prayer.
He imagines someone plugging the soda machine
and all the cans fall out like Christmas,
half hearted cheers going up in the lobby
as the movie burns through television snow
and just when he's getting to the really good part
the preacher turns into Mel Tormé and
forget about the blood of the lamb,
would you like to swing on a star?

III.   RISING AND FALLING

Hours in the room next door
they've been banging the bed senseless.
Each time he knocks on the wall
someone screams another promise
it won't be too much longer.
Nights like this he tries to picture
every angle two bodies could hope for,
flesh slapping flesh until finally
the tide in the blood goes out.

In his bed, brushing against sleep,
he imagines the whole hotel rising
and falling in hot flashes,
knows anything can pass, one time,
for compassion. Tonight
his roomkey could swell in the lock
until it turns into the key to the city.
The man crawling up and down the hall
might be the mailman with years of letters
come to beg forgiveness.
The curtains blowing into his room
are someone's arms reaching as far as they can,
the closest he's come to a derelict promise
of love and what happens all night in its name.

And still the room next door's on springs.
He wonders if anyone will walk out alive.

The last lights in his eyes give out
and in the dark he listens to his own heart
pounding the thin walls of his life.
He could teach his heart a lesson
on all the good it does,
how it's better off wishing for something
to snap: some thread of nerve, a leg,
the bed caving in. This is the prayer
it can't be too much longer, the prayer
he thinks one night he'll put his heart in
and the answer when it comes that time
won't be completely wrong.

Dancing Down the Circus

Just wish one thing was different. Wish I'd married and had a daughter to treat real good. Would've called her Rose.

FOR OLD BARNEY

I.

Around this place so long he knows
the Snake Woman's given name,
knows after 37 years it's done with mirrors,
this way his face still shines
on nights wheeling into dawn.
Each town he rolls into he's coming home.
Sleeping days in the head trailer
while the midway swells like a river in storm.
Waking, rolling smokes with the lions. He's king
of this jumble of canvas, poles, and wires.
He knows every stress and gesture
giving the circus shape.
The freaks tell him secrets they keep
from people who pay to be told.
Each clown lets him in
on a new way to grow old.

II.

Somewhere in the middle of all those years
he watched a tiny girl in red

trickle down the midway
and he followed, calling her names
he loved. All night he imagined
a daughter whose name was a flower.
While the townies danced the circus down
for a handful of coins,
he went to the last tent standing, kissed
the girl he held tight as breath
to his chest, and tossed her high
up past the tops of cages, past
the silent high wire until her tiny legs
touched canvas and kicked through
and they both saw stars silvering the sky
on the first real night of their lives.

III.

Tonight wind whips the tent flags
another color. A few drops of rain
and it's a different country,
tearing down this last tent in a storm.
He dries out in a neon after-hours corner
where he tells his daughter's fortune
to strangers. A few more drinks
and he glues his eyes to the door.
Each time a woman whispers in
his heart quickens up his throat and goes out.

• •

Rose, a name that grows too big
for the hollow in his chest.

Rose, Rose, a woman finally
perfectly formed on his lips.

Traveller's Advisory

Why does it seem it's always a woman,
when you're driving between towns on the road
trying to figure out the radio
stations fading in, out at every turn
until you finally get some painful song,
who drives your mind to taverns and to drink?

Sometimes you're convinced it will work: drink
and you'll see things aren't half-bad. The woman
will grow quiet, drift away with the song.
But you know when you get back to the road
it won't be nearly hard enough to turn
the dials, bring life back to the radio.

You remember times with the radio
broken you sang loud and blamed it on drink.
It didn't matter. Later on you turned
and turned in sleep, couldn't shake the woman
from your brain and that night was a long road
winding into sunrise, another song.

You might get lucky. Not everything's song.
Take comfort in the words the radio
doles out in wavelengths up and down the road.
A slow sweep of the dial and you can drink
it in: Peoria, a madwoman
guns down a clerk, tired of waiting her turn

in line. In some small town the mayor turns
red, grabs his heart. He's reaching for a song

if you could see him. He knows no woman
hurts like this. These aches on the radio
send people everywhere some place to drink,
to sit and say this next one's for the road,

to think about what's farther down that road,
Each day something's left behind, a dream turns
back into straw. No wonder people drink.
No wonder people rock themselves with song.
They don't tell you that on the radio
but you learned it along with the plural of *woman*.

Tonight you take this road without a song
as towns turn to static on the radio.
Miles back a woman pours herself a drink.

Letter from Eureka, Nevada

In these hills there is
nothing to fall back on.
1890 pushed the bottom out of silver
and the mines closed quick as sprung traps.
The smart ones figured a way to escape
with a gleam still left in their eyes.
Others less resourceful stayed,
staked to the land. And I swear
there's breathing in these hills, whispers
from the cemeteries mimicking sounds
of pickaxe and hammer working stone.

I'm staying with a man who's learned
a language his grandfather never spoke.
He denies the stories of black smoke
that belched from the smelters,
filling the air with a smell
of money and time well-spent.
He plays cards in the opera house,
songless for years. Goes to church
to earn another living. Pays when he can
for his groceries in cash.
He says it's holding on
to the little things that's hard.
I sit porched with him on late afternoons
while he waits for his reign as honorary mayor.
He points to the hills and calls them
dark animals ringing the town in, tight.
In his sleep he talks his way past them:

• •

he is writing a letter.
How life is good.
How once in a while
what he loves is strong enough
to rearrange the grey.

Mormon Graveyard, Utah Night

FOR ALAN SMITH

Up P Street where the houses quit
the road backs off from a church.
You say the first thing I should know is
past that spire we're on our own,
can't say what brings you back each time
over this fence, past the guard in the window
staring through his sleep.

Uphill, and hoot owls rattle in a chill
late autumn pounds into these mountains.
Younger, I believed in
my whistle past graveyards, a way I knew
to stay alive. Now
sitting on this bench we're singing
Devil Moon, looking over Salt Lake City
shivering in a coat of light.

Flowers browning in a gravepot speak
a recent death and we can't decide:
someone shot, mistaken in the Bel-Air Tap
or a man on the tracks behind the Rescue Mission
waiting for a train. I'll guess anything
except going into all this,
quiet as a life, in sleep. Across the valley
spotlights flare then dim, beginning their sweep.
You tell me Kennecott Copper, wait for me
to say that's all I wondered.

But I want to know why anyone
named the road winding through here Main,
why here the wind dies as soon as it rises.

It must be the view that keeps you coming back,
something to hold onto as you lose the city
light by light.
And taking the easy walk downhill,
huddled in our jackets, you whisper
it's an accident we're trampling the dead,
trying their names on our lips
and throwing them off into Utah night.

We'll be ready if the guard's head starts awake
out of the one bad dream he knows:
somebody crazed, up on the mountain
stealing bodies or a kiss
or the last good draught of fall.
We've been there, in that dream.
We'll tell him we've just come back from the dead
and there's no stopping us now.

Close to Home

I. THE CLEAN PLATE

In the restaurant a mother gets tough
with her small daughter, orders her
to clean her plate. As soon as she says
look at that man over there
I know it's bad advice.
I'm slumping at the counter,
drunk on breakfast specials.
The waitress is filling her pad
with my hunger, passing notes
I can't read to the cook. I want
to get beyond her good-for-business smile.
To roll the cook out of the kitchen.
Want to tell the mother and the daughter
and all of them it isn't always like this.
But we're past that, midnight, no time
to explain. In its kettle the soup of the day
changes color. I pay the waitress
for everything that's happened.
I take my change and buy three mints,
a postcard, an unbreakable comb.
By now the mother is probably coaxing,
promising a clean plate as a sign
you'll never want for anything.
If she could see me walking down the street,
she might point me out again and
tell her daughter another story like
it takes so little to be happy, not saying

sometimes when we lie down in the dark
we have to arm ourselves
to the teeth with even that.

II. THE HOTEL

The owner's out from behind the desk
and brandishing my key, saying
the elevator's lost between floors for years.
No one around and she walks me past
the prayer plants and flowering cactus,
walks me up the stairs, slow.
She means every step, every once-
in-a-lifetime story.
By the time we reach the top
I know when all the trains came through,
that by dinner every day was paid for.
Even when the lobby mirror filled with people
she could stare into the crowd,
no trouble finding the face
with a few years on it she'd admit to.
From my door she points through the dark
to a room where they shot part of a movie
once. She brought them coffee
and they thanked her. She saw the movie twice.

Tonight in my sleep she rides the elevator,
humming over the hum of machinery,
rolling back the door and stepping out
with a bounce in her two good legs.
The flowers on her dress still fresh.
Knocking on doors to ask if
everything's all right.

                    I wake up
and get on the phone. When she answers
after one ring I remember what's lost.
I can see the desk, the ledgers
talking in their sleep behind her.
My voice feels dumb on the line
and ends up asking where's the ice, adding
I think the view is wonderful. And
the clean sheets. And the towels hung just so.

III.   THE SUICIDE

Slow going out of town. A man on the bridge
holds up his fists and promises
to jump. He doesn't know
this is the schoolboy's threat,
that serious students think
flecks of brain on walls or maybe
a stove where nothing's cooking.
The crowd out here is dying for him
to make a better show of it. The priest
is talking willful acts against the self
with the cop rerouting traffic.
The cop knows better, knows whether
it's winter coming or the Chevy died or love,
it's all the same.
If I thought I knew more about
what the river could take away,
I would say let me talk to him.
I watch in the rearview until I lose sight.
I go one more set of lights, turn left
and hope the right direction.
I'll crawl onto the shoulder if I get tired
or when I reach the roadblocks in my head,
a routine check that won't take long.
You're not who we're looking for,
and I'll pretend relief:
no bodies on the back seat.
No gloves on the dash. Not even

a flashlight in my wide eyes.
Tonight I'm ready to confess to anything
and they're letting me go on,
getting away with what's left between
this town and the next one,
between the river and the closest star to home.

We Never Close

Our Special Services manager is Helen Waite.
If you want special service, go to Helen Waite.
　　　　　—taped on the wall in Tony's Chophouse

Some nights you need to get into the car and drive
until you find it, that familiar hash-house glow
that means Open All Night in Spokane or Hackensack
or anywhere between. But it's the brazen nature
of the promise spelled out in the window
that keeps you coming back: WE NEVER CLOSE.
Times like this nothing softer, nothing less
will do. You're a veteran of the edge of town,
an old hand at the middle of nowhere. Sometimes
you wake up and you're living your life
in the static between stations, between the prayer
and the answer: one lover and another. Between
jobs or novels or whole religions. You're looking
for something to hold onto between right now and
sunrise, two bad dreams, and some nights it takes
more than a feather pillow to sustain you.
There's something in the way the waitress
yells her order to some guy five feet away,
the same short-order man you always see, same beefy
tattoo of a heart and words the years have finally blurred
into the vaguely Universal. Maybe *Born To* something. Maybe
something *Love*. Or the name of a ship that went down.
Or a woman. What matters is he's here unflinchingly
for you. He'll do Pig In A Blanket or Pie In The Sky

and even his mistakes with eggs are redeemed somewhere
in his imagination: Adam & Eve In A Padded Room,
Adam & Eve In Hell. With his spatula and maniacal grin
he always puts the fear of someone's God into you good.

Tonight the waitress recites a list of everything
she's out of. It's not much, compared to yours,
that litany of the gone and the going you sang softly
back to the radio. When she asks what you're having,
you know the obvious answer: *another one of*
those nights. But instead you take a guess out loud:
whatever's good, something you haven't had in a while.
And you're amazed that she can make it sound so special
for a minute, her own apotheosis of one more order
of the Usual. Your soup turns into Yesterday, Today, And
Always. Pin A Rose On It, and your hamburger's blessed
with a gigantic slice of raw. Coffee—Make It Sweet,
Sweetness And Light. And you're so lightheaded
with wonder you could almost ask her what she's doing
when she gets off. From where you sit it's hard
to tell the color of her eyes, but you'd have to guess
some shade of blue, the local color here:
Blue Plate Special, smoke on the rise from a dozen ashtrays,
the cop sweet-talking another Danish he won't pay for,
an entire row of songs in the jukebox, the blue-streak
chatter of the woman on the pay phone fingering the dark
blue bruise on the back of her neck, and suddenly
any blue you brought here with you pales in comparison.
• •

It hurts just looking at it and thinking how
you'd hold up under that kind of wear, a pain
you could actually point to and insist *here's where* . . .
It All Began, or Went Bad, or Came To An End—
depending on who'll listen. Say you can tell
from the swelling it's no accident: runs too deep.
One night on the way in or out of the kitchen
the love she thought she had coming turned into
A Sudden Blur of Hurt. After who knows how long
driving alone, this call is finally her way to
send it back. It's hard to make out very many
of her words, but you're jealous of whoever's
anywhere down the line to hear them.
Even if she rehearsed every mile of the ride out here,
she still doesn't sound sure, doesn't know how to say
no more, don't wait up, she won't be back, ever.
You want to see her slam that receiver into its cradle,
want it to sound like the irreversible thunk
of a car meeting something alive in the road.

The waitress drops a steaming plate
at the empty stool next to you. *Here's the lady's*
she says to no one in particular, and you realize
she could be talking to you again. Maybe
she's lumped you and the woman on the phone together
in the legion of the bruised, the day-old,
the bottom of the pot. You're stuck in the middle
between denying everything and confessing, when she winks
and out of nowhere assures you *it's working.*

No matter what she has in mind, you'd like to believe her.
She seems so sure that nothing else has broken down
or gone wrong since you got here. You'd like to take her home
where she could talk you through those days
of more dull ache than you can say.
And whatever hunger drove you here in the first place,
whatever you wanted so badly you could taste it,
you haven't seen anything yet.
Ask the woman now trying to convince the operator
this whole thing's been a mistake, one very long
wrong number. Ask the waitress who's already
running a hot bath in her mind.

Miles from here you'll be alone in the shower singing
whatever's left of your heart out, trying to remember
how it goes, this exalting of the ordinary.
If the night's not good enough the first time,
send it back: *Pin A Rose On It*. Yell out of love
at the top of your lungs if you have to: *Make It
Sweetness. Make It Light.*
And in the steamed-up bathroom mirror,
a little fainter maybe, but right where you wrote it
the last time: WE NEVER CLOSE. You'll see your own face
somewhere in that promise, and you'll be just barely
back in business again. Sometimes you stay open
so long it hurts. Ask the waitress who'll be no good
for anything tomorrow. Ask the woman down to her last
dime of crying. Or the short-order man. Put yourself
in his place, bent over the grill. The long haul

he's in it for, elbow-deep in another desperate creation.
Doomed to a life without sleep when some idiot
years ago unlocked the door and threw away the key.
He's logged so much time waiting for relief
that if someone punched in now and put on an apron,
he'd have to believe he was seeing things.

You'll be shivering in your towel,
afraid to admit you still can't help feeling
that no matter how long you've been living like this,
someone's going even longer out of her way tonight,
that any minute she'll walk back in from out of the blue.
She's spent all night working up the nerve.
It's what she wants, if you can find it in your heart.
Her hair will be the sheen of brown you remember
and her neck, perfect eggshell smooth.
Not a single wince in her body. Suddenly it hurts
just imagining it. Knocks the wind clean out of you
and drops you cold where you live.

You open your eyes and she's really here. Your waitress,
laying down everything you once hoped for on the counter,
and by now you're wishing it was something else completely.
She doesn't need to tell you: it's not working anymore.
She looks at the plate of eggs next to you,
the one the grill man's made up like a face
growing colder every minute: *I guess your friend's not
very hungry.* And you can't remember
what you ever saw in her. You don't remember asking

for any of this, but here it comes anyway.
With your name on it. Yesterday. Today. Always.
And for the first time in your lifetime of places
just like this, you can see the cockeyed wisdom
in the Hav-A-Hank handkerchiefs for sale
behind the counter, in the measured doses of Bromo
hanging over the cartoon outline of a man
with the fizz already gone out of him.
They're on hand for the sadness and the burning.
Tonight you understand
what you couldn't as a kid in the daylight
when all you could take seriously after lunch
was finally buying one of those unbreakable combs.
Hard to believe, but there it was, bent over nearly double
on its cardboard display: *Sweetheart—The Only One
You'll Ever Need.* One dime and it was yours
and it would last, that preposterous strength more than
you'd ever need. That good breeze blowing in
through every window in the wide-open world.

PART IV.

Like Nothing You've Ever Seen

Don't be a luddy duddy! Don't be a moon calf!
Don't be a jabbernowl! You're not those, are you?
        —W.C. Fields, *The Bank Dick*

This Book Belongs to Susan Someone

*(on finding a copy of a friend's book, heavily marked and underlined,
in a second-hand bookshop)*

FOR BILL KLOEFKORN

It's only her version of what you were trying to do
yourself: getting it down on paper, the right words
that will say it so it stays said that way forever,
whatever you once imagined *it* might be.
Reading her inky notations from this distance,
it's hard to tell. So often it seems to be her word
flush against yours, and who's to say, false modesty aside,
which one of you deserves believing more?
Surely once she must have had the profound feeling
she could think of better things to stay awake this late for.
The way I see it, she's up all night in bed
listening to the sound of your words in her mouth,
that figurative kiss she really wants no part of.
But she's so desperate to make out anything, no matter how
self-explanatory, that she writes *sad* here, *disappointing*
there. Turn the page and now it's *frustration*
all over the place, and it's absolutely palpable,
her side of it. Another page and it's raining
metaphor and *symbol* from a cloud of wishful thinking,
out of the blue felt-tip of habit pressing down
until she's finally writing *I don't get it:* the poem
like a joke, the love, the sleep she truly needs.

• •

Because she knows what you've suspected for some time:
there will be a test on this, though hers will come
more tangibly and sooner. And while she shakes her head,
angry that she has to provide for this distraction
she never asked into her life, worried
she'll run out of coffee before enough of it sinks in,
she's writing her own anxious heart out
until it casts a shadow, takes on a life of its own, here
at the end of your book. I'm reading between the lines
when I suppose her motives were as pure as yours
because that's where she's put that small part of herself
trying to wish some connection into existence,
some sudden interstate that might finally replace
the slower backroads, those precarious hairpin turns
between the brain and the heart. It's obvious she's stuck
in the dark again. You've got to admire her for whistling.

By now her roommate's probably asleep, murmuring
in some dreamy *ur*-language that existed before the need
to speak it, before the urge to write its imperfections down.
Awake, it's trickier business, this saying
so deliberately what we can only hope means anything.
Especially when we're at it this late, weighing words
until they somehow seem to matter, until
we look at them again in the next day's excruciating light
and realize mostly we stayed up all night for not nearly enough.

And although she might have come to hate the very sound
of your name, the thought of everything you put her through,

I bet in other ways she's far too reasonable, too good
to be still carrying a grudge. More likely that night's
the farthest thing from her mind. Even if you can picture her
in the room full of people where she is tonight,
and even if she pauses between the drinks and dinner
to whisper a few words in her lover's ear, don't think
for a minute it has anything to do with you.
She's come a long way to get to this place in her life
where finally she's happy almost beyond words,
and these days if she knows any disappointment,
it's nothing she can say. If she'd had to rely on
the fragile wings of song, she'd still be back in her dormitory
sweating out those hours again before she passed her test,
but just barely. And you wherever you are,
with your own frantic pages of notes to get back to,
another night drunk down to the cold bottom of the cup,
imagining an even better poem somewhere in the margins
of the best you can do right now,
you know how that one goes.

What Other People Think

I do care about you, a lot, but I also care about what other people think.
                    —overheard while passing a phone booth

Some cells live good lives
and never make it to the brain.
They settle in the thighs, the fingertips,
the back's small curving
and you like the way it feels,
these thousands of small secrets
telling themselves. Sometimes
you catch yourself,
your smile well-aimed and running deep
before too many eyebrows rise.

What other people think are ways of saying
they've seen it coming,
they've thought it over: no good can come.
Now they make you their special concern,
the smallest favor they know.

This time tell them yes, it's everything
they've imagined all along.
Tell them what's folded in a whisper
could destroy a city block,
that the space between your heart
and what comes next is falling off.
Say it's true your heart goes out
when you least expect, flexing its muscle.
••

There's a message passed on
with the first cell's splitting,
a story opening wide like a mouth
that comforts children when their beds are small,
that later brings them, older, to their knees.

Back to Life

Many of these reports have aspects in common: bright lights, unearthly music, a floating sensation followed by a view of the physical body from somewhere above . . . These subjects tell of seeing familiar people who'd died before them reaching out reassuringly. Some mention a being dressed in light, exuding an indescribable warmth. And before they know it, they're in their own bodies again. But what happened to them seemed to make profound changes in the rest of their lives.

> —from an article on people who've died and lived to
> tell about their "life-after-life" experiences

I.

When the room went blinding white I closed my eyes.
Then the music came, the kind that's piped in
anywhere you don't need music,
and I could have been strolling the grocery aisles,
wavering in Canned Goods, frantic in Cold Cuts,
finally breaking down at the Checkout and buying
more gum than a country could chew.
But when I opened my eyes I found out
I was in some private elevator rising in the dark
and I couldn't for the life of me remember
asking for a hospital room like this one,
the bill they'd send me going through the roof.
When I stepped off into thin air
and looked down at myself in bed,
I could clearly see I'd gone too far.
I saw the doctor panic, rip apart my gown
as if he still could pull me through.
I remember wishing he'd give up

and hand over whatever's left to the nurse.
I'd found a whole new point of view
where her harsh plainness curved into beauty.
I wanted her to blow me a kiss,
to be an angel and quote Plato's *dreamless sleep*.
I doubt it even crossed her mind. I doubt
that's what she wrote down on my chart
when the doctor shook his head,
when all negotiations ended in his eyes.
No kiss and no philosophy.
Just ordinary, down-to-earth decorum.
I'd have settled for a lilting *bought the farm*.

What really killed me was those Mellowfinger Strings.
Absolutely heartless on the part of God.
No chords being wrenched from an organ,
no saxophone swinging low.
In a world more perfect, this one or the Next,
Monk's *Misterioso* would be the way to go.

II.

My idea of a Great Beyond
would be not running into anyone who knew me.
No family. No friends.
Just a roomkey, an assumed name, a weakness
in the knees and a sly wink from the nightclerk,
his promise to keep this out of the news.
In a truly Great Beyond my personal angel

would be W.C. Fields in slippers and gin.
We'd sing together loud nights in the hall.
But I don't remember getting any final wish.
I would have asked for too much one last time.
What I got was the Obligatory Beyond:
people I'd somehow managed to outlive
on parade through a long home movie of the dead.

I saw my grainy father waving for me to follow him
as if he knew some secret shortcut back to town.
I suppose he meant it as a gesture of solace,
but that far out-of-focus I couldn't be sure.
I remember him calling me to supper like that
when I was young enough to think
I was too young to die,
and my fatal mistake every time was that I went
into the interminable dining room
where I looked up once in a while from my plate
as I picked bones clean in the silence
and watched the after-supper daylight-saving
ball-throwing sunlight slip away in the dark.

I saw my fourth grade teacher, her hair even more
ethereally blue. One day after school
she warned me every inadvertent burp and missed report
was being written down in my Permanent Record.
Her low-key blackmail scared me into line
until my brother told me it was only a hoax
passed on from one year to the next.

Seeing her again after so long, I wondered
what she'd really done with those hundreds of notes
full of undying love I meant for Debbie Fuller.

At this rate it was bound to happen:
Lou Chambers, overweight neighbor I dreaded,
still pulling pins from invisible grenades
and diving to the ground, his moronic introduction
to yet another story from the Big One, WW II.
The truth in his life-and-death blather
would fit on the head of one pin.

And what I thought might be the fabled Being
of Light turned out to be Small Heart Cooper
fresh from his counter at Third Avenue Sweets,
still all fidget and malice, shining
a mirror into my eyes like he'd finally do
when I played pinball on one dime all afternoon.
I couldn't see anything through the glare
and he'd laugh while I drained down the middle.

Please don't believe anyone who says
life flashes in front of your eyes.
At best it's a dull ache behind them. Or maybe
you're only imagining what really isn't there.
It could be Scrooge's gruel, your own last meal,
mere chemicals the brain lets go for entertainment,
to pass whatever time it thinks is left.

I say go out and buy any theory
that might make you feel better when you're back
to your old self, still wild-eyed in bed
hours later when the nurse brings dinner
and you're trying to convince yourself that
no matter what you've just been through,
there must be a Great Beyond somewhere, or at least
a Reasonable Beyond. Until even the mysterious
pudding on your tray is a good omen:

it will be like nothing
you've ever seen in your life.

III.

Since I've been back I've heard a lot of talk,
how I'm supposed to know an inner peace so deep
it can't be fathomed, some tranquility
huge and inexpressible as sky. I'm here
to tell you what I know so far
is only crackpot love and admiration.

My friend read a book he swears is true
and suddenly he's a scholar of the Other Side
and other people who've returned
ecstatic with versions of serene eternal life.
I try to tell him that's a crock or else
they've been misquoted. He can't believe it

when I say my nerves are ringing off the hook.
From everything he's read, calm's bound to come.

What comes today is a letter from someone in Wyoming
who claims he's been legally dead 18 times
and wants to start a club of people just like us.
He says if I join right away
he'll send me the name of this woman he knows
who whispers sweet nothings on the astral plane.
I think I'd rather learn the Secret Handshake.
I think this whole thing's badly out of hand.

What I've been through is a far cry from a miracle.
Think of your own emotional close call,
your spirit worn down to bare filament
and your heart gone dry, running on fumes,
on one too many day's accumulation of white light
with no real color in it.
Like everyone, you waited for the dark
before you came apart completely.
You closed your eyes, and it was touch and go.

Didn't you feel each cell in your body
sweating out your life?
And secretly you cheered them on.
You thought it wouldn't hurt to see
how far things could go wrong.

Be grateful there were no machines plugged in
to measure the implosions.
You would have seen your heart and brain reduced
to humming parallel lines.

And wasn't that the first time you noticed
yourself, through a fluke of genuine perception,
lying absolutely still, waiting for something big
to happen? And didn't it happen
it was a small eternity of waiting, and for nothing
you were counting on, nothing larger than life?

You just did what anyone would have done
in your position. Sure, it would be nice
to say you tried something more heroic, like
looking your dying straight in the face
and knocking out its teeth.
You admitted you were scared. But not to death.
It's no wonder you backed down, sneaked away
and caught your breath. Came slowly
to your senses, your bones lining up days on end
to take back their familiar weight.

So you tell me.
Did you feel any calmer in your body than before,
worry less about losing your hair?
Were you nonchalant in your shower
when the water went cold without warning?

Did you stare down the shivering length of your life
and find anything so good
you never knew you had it?

Because when we come back, it's always
right where we left off: the middle
of a night, a room where the phone never rings
or it never stops ringing.
And now that we have both sides of the story,
we'd rather forget everything we know,
start over and see how it goes this time.
But we know too much. So what we ask is
another day in oblivion's good graces
before it all comes back to us.

New Year's Eve Letter to Friends

Every year the odds are stacked against it
turning out the way you'd like:
a year of smooth, a year of easy smile,
a year like a lake you could float on,
looking up at a blue year of soothing sky.

Mostly the letters you're expecting never come.
Lovers walk out and keep on going
and in no time they're no friends of yours.
Mostly, the sheer weight of days
gone awfully wrong: a tire blown out,
someone's heart caving in,
the hole worn finally through the roof.
Sometimes it's only a few tenacious cells
digging in against complete dissolve.
The smallest strand of DNA, stretched thin
over thousands of years, goes taut
and finally holds.

I've watched men at the Mission staring out
into the middle distance,
putting up with the latest version of salvation,
all the time wondering just
how long until the bowl and spoon.
They've been around enough to know
the good part's always saved for last and
there's no promise they won't make to get there.
Each year cuts our lives down to size,

to something we can almost use. So we find it
somewhere in our hearts: another ring shows up
when we lay open the cross-section.
One more hard line in the hand
spreading slowly out of its clench.

It used to be the world was so small
you could walk out to the end of it
and back in a single day. Now it seems
to take all year to make it mostly back.
And so this is for my friends all over:
a new year. Year the longshot comes home.
The year letters pour in, full of the good word
that never got as far as you before.
The year lovers come to know a good thing
when they find it in the press of familiar flesh.
Walk out onto the planet tonight. Even the moon
is giving back your share of borrowed light
and you take it back, in the name of everything
you can't take back in your life.
Imagine yourself filling with it,
letting yourself go and floating
through the skeleton trees to your place
at the top of the sky.

And here's the best part, coming last,
just after all your practiced shows of faith.
Even now, while you're still salvaging

what passes for resolve.
Remember this, no matter what else happens:
this year you'll never go without.
It's no small thing you've been in line for,
this bowl and spoon passed finally to you.